If You Had a Nose like an Elephant's Trunk

by Marion Dane Bauer

illustrations by Susan Winter

Holiday House / New York

Text copyright © 2001 by Marion Dane Bauer
Illustrations copyright © 2001 by Susan Winter
All Rights Reserved
Printed in the United States of America
The text typeface is Garamond #3.
The illustrations were painted in watercolor.
www.holidayhouse.com
First Edition

Library of Congress Cataloging-in-Publication Data
Bauer, Marion Dane.
If you had a nose like an elephant's trunk / by Marion Dane Bauer;
illustrations by Susan Winter.—1st ed.
p. cm.
Summary: A young girl imagines what it would be like
to have a tongue like a snapping turtle, feet like a fly,
a tail like a lizard, or cheeks like a chipmunk.
ISBN 0-8234-1589-9 (hardcover)
[1. Animals—Fiction.
2. Body, Human—Fiction.]
I. Winter, Susan, ill. II. Title.

PZ7.B3262 If 2001
[E]—dc21   00-032005

For Cullen Baird Bauer
M. D. B.

To Lulu and Jessica,
who have the prettiest noses
on the planet
S. W.

If you had a nose

like an elephant's trunk,
you could make it rain inside the house.
You could pick up your toys with your nose.
You would never, ever need a snorkel.

If you had feet like a fly's,
you could walk up the wall
and take a nap on the ceiling.

If you had a tongue like a snapping turtle's,
you could go fishing without a rod and reel.

If you had jaws like a snake's,
you could swallow a bowling ball.
And if the bowling ball were nutritious,
you wouldn't have to eat again
for weeks and weeks.

If you had spinnerets
like a spider's,
you could sail, sail away
on every breezy day.

If you could change color like a chameleon,
you could never be found
in a game of hide-and-seek.

If you had the legs of a flea,
you could leap over your house with glee!

If you had wings like an eagle's,
you could climb, climb into the sky.
If you had eyes like an eagle's,
you could peer back down
and see an ant walking
across the sidewalk.

If you had a mouth
like a mosquito's,
you could get
a sip of milk
without ever
opening the carton.

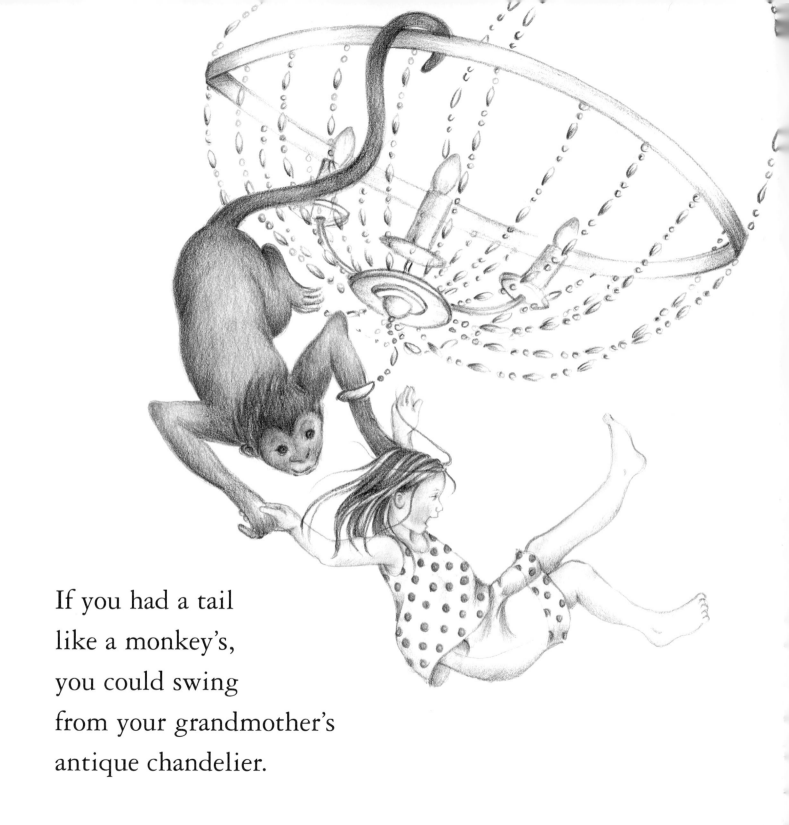

If you had a tail
like a monkey's,
you could swing
from your grandmother's
antique chandelier.

If you had a tail like a horse's,
you could brush the flies
from your friends' faces.

If you had a tail like a porcupine's,
the bullies would all leave town.

If you had a tail
like a lizard's,
you could never
be caught
in a game of tag.

If you had any kind of tail at all,
you would have to cut holes
in all your pants!

If you had cheeks
like a chipmunk's,
you would never need
a lunch box.

Bus
Stop

If you slept like a cow,
you could catch a few winks
while you stood waiting for the bus.

If you slept like a shark,
you could nap while you swam.

If you slept like a swift,
you could fly through your own dreams.

But you have your own nose,

your own legs, your own mouth.

You can leap and run and crouch.

You can hold
a dandelion seed
in your fingers
and you can
lift a stone.

You can smell rain

and you can lick ice cream

and you can see your father's face.

You can sleep snugly
in your own sweet bed.

Because you are made
just to be you.
And we're so glad!